Y has a long ....

*To the memory of my mother who
always found time to explain why.*

A Red Fox Book

Published by Arrow Books Limited
20 Vauxhall Bridge Road, London SW1V 2SA

An imprint of the Random Century Group

London Melbourne Sydney Auckland
Johannesburg and agencies throughout the world

First published in Great Britain by Blackie and Son Ltd 1989

Red Fox edition 1991

© Errol Lloyd 1989

The right of Errol Lloyd to be identified
as the author/illustrator of this work has been
asserted by him in accordance with the
Copyright, Designs and Patents Act, 1988

Made and printed in Great Britain

ISBN 0 09 971520 1

Y has a long tail

Errol Lloyd

RED FOX

'It's time to go home, Lenny,' said Dad.

'Why?' asked Lenny.
'Because you must be getting tired,'
said Dad.

'Why?' asked Lenny.
'Because you've been playing for a long time,' said Dad.

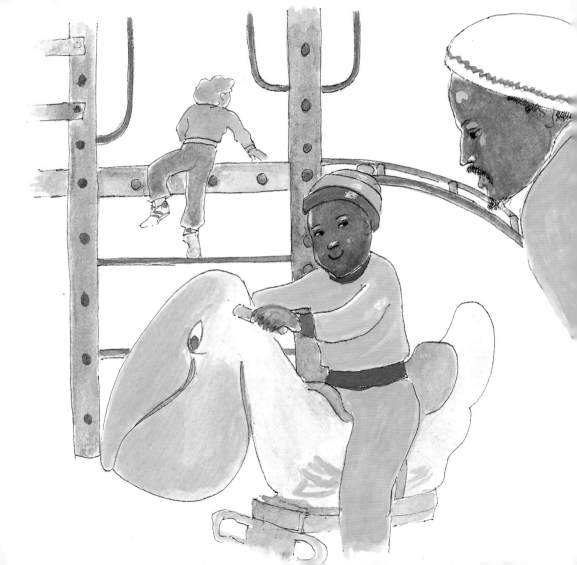

'Why?' asked Lenny.
'Because you've got tons of energy,'
said Dad.

'Why?' asked Lenny.
'Because you eat lots and lots of food,'
said Dad.

'Why?' asked Lenny.
'Because you have a very big tummy,' said Dad.

'Why?' asked Lenny.
'Because you are very greedy,' said
Dad.

'Why?' asked Lenny.
'Because you get very very very hungry,' said Dad.

'Why?' asked Lenny.
'Because you are growing and learning all the time,' said Dad.

'Why?' asked Lenny.
'So you can learn to put on your own coat,' said Dad.

'Why?' asked Lenny.
'Because it's time to go home,' said Dad.

'Why?' asked Lenny.
'Because Y has a long tail,' said Dad.

Other titles in the Red Fox picture book series (incorporating Beaver Books)